BENJIE AND THE FLOOD

Frances Walter
Violet T. Pearson

ACCENT BOOKS
Denver, Colorado

Second Printing, 1981

ACCENT BOOKS
A division of Accent Publications, Inc.
12100 W. Sixth Avenue
P.O. Box 15337
Denver, Colorado 80215

Library of Congress Catalog Card Number: 78-65063
ISBN: 0-89636-017-2

Benjie and the Flood

Benjie and the Flood

Benjie Beaver really liked to feel the rain when the drops fell on his thick fur. It didn't make much difference to Benjie or his brother or his two sisters when it rained. They were wet so much of the time as they played in the water of their pond.

Father and Mother Beaver made their pond. They built a dam across a stream. As the water backed up, there was a nice beaver pond where they could build their safe lodge. Nearby they built a pile of branches with green leaves on them. This feed pile kept them supplied with food.

But when the rain began to come down too hard and the wind would blow too much, the beavers' dam might be weakened. Then their beautiful home would be in danger!

This is what happened to the Beaver family the winter the flood came to where they lived. This started some exciting experiences for all of them. As you follow their adventures, you will come to love Benjie and his family. You will learn that it is a good thing for families to work together.

The story of Benjie and his family shows us many things about God's wonderful creation. God made each kind of animal different so they could live their own special way. Each animal has his own knowledge of what is danger for him. He knows how to avoid it. God gave him this wisdom.

Animals know how to talk to each other. Of course, they do not talk in people's language. But when we pretend that they talk in our language, we can learn about the ways of beavers and other animals.

As you read Benjie's story, you may want to thank God for your own family. Ask Him how you can help make it a happy Christian family.

Benjie Gets Angry

"This is the most wonderful part of the world!" said Benjie. "Look at the beautiful trees. Smell the crisp air. I can hardly wait to see our lodge."

Benjamin Beaver and his family were only a few miles from home. They had been away all summer on a vacation exploring other streams and seeing many different kinds of animals. Now they were getting very excited as they saw familiar places.

"I guess everyone thinks his home is the best," agreed Father Beaver. "But I have to admit I will be glad to get back and check everything around our lodge."

"Oh, my, let's not take time to talk," said Mother. "Let's just swim as fast as we can to get home quickly." The water rippled as six beaver heads bobbed along in the water—father and mother and four beaver kits.

Suddenly Benjie called out, "There it is! There it is! Our home!" At last they had arrived. The Beaver family swam around their lodge. They hardly knew what to do first.

Mother hurried inside to see if it was all right. Father went all around the pond dropping his scent so other water animals would know he was home. Benjie, his brother and two sisters, swam all around the pond. They dived in, inspected things underwater, and popped up again.

Then they all swam over to check the dam. The dam was very important to the Beaver family. Long ago they built the dam with sticks and mud across a stream. It forced the water in the stream to stop flowing. Then the water made them a nice beaver pond.

Soon Father said, "It looks as if it was a quiet summer at home. There must not have been any heavy rains. Our dam is in good condition. I can't find one weak spot."

"Maybe the rains are late getting here," said Mother. "We ought to add some sticks and mud just the same to make it stronger."

"We will," said Father. "But we do not have to hurry to do that. There are many other things we must do to get ready for winter."

"What will we have to do?" asked Benjie. "We have our house built, and the dam is fine."

"What do you think we are going to eat all winter?" asked Mother.

"Why, there are plenty of trees around," replied Benjie. "We can always cut down something to eat."

"I see you have something to learn about winter," said Mother. "Do you know our whole pond will be covered with ice? You will not be able to get out of it."

"The trees and bushes will all be stiff and bare," added Father. "They will be hard to cut down and will not taste good."

"I do not think you would like to work in the snow, either," answered Mother.

"What will we do for food?" asked Benjie's sister.

"We have to work now and get it cut down," answered Father. "We need to cut enough trees to last six hungry beavers for the whole winter!"

Father showed them a place near the lodge. It would be easy to come out one of the runways from the lodge and get food from the feed pile. The water would keep the wood fresh and unfrozen.

Soon they were all busy working. The

forest rang with the chop-chop of six pairs of long orange-colored teeth as they bit into the wood. Then a mighty thwack with a tail would warn when a tree was ready to fall.

Every time Benjie cut down a tree he had to stop and eat the tenderest twigs. "Stop eating our winter food," called one of his sisters. "Can't you ever stop eating?"

"I only took a little snack," replied Benjie. "If I cut down the tree, can't I eat some of it?"

The other kits watched Benjie. They decided to play a trick on him. The next time Benjie started to eat, his brother took hold of the branch and pulled it away.

Benjie jumped up and down and stamped his feet, squeaking with anger. Then he grabbed the branch and pulled it back.

The others laughed at him. Benjie wasn't usually cross, but he didn't like his food taken away from him. It didn't make him feel better when they all laughed at him.

Benjie still felt very unhappy inside.

"Aw, Benjie," said his sister. "We're sorry."

Just then Mother called them. "Come on, you kits," she said. "It is time to take a quick swim and then off to bed."

Benjie, his brother and two sisters dived into the water. They had a fast game of tag, then went to their bedroom in the lodge. They snuggled close together and went to sleep, happy to be back safely in their home. Benjie was glad he didn't feel angry anymore.

Benjie Tells Stories

"Time to wake up, you sleepy beavers," called Mother. "Father is already out cutting down trees to add to the feed pile. He needs our help."

The four kits stretched and yawned. One thing for sure, it didn't take them long to wake up. As they swam out of the lodge into the pond, the cool water made them wide-awake. They dived to the bottom to see how the feed pile was coming along. It certainly didn't look very big. When Benjie thought of how much he liked to eat, he knew he would have to work harder.

The young beavers were soon busy cutting the trees near the pond. If the trees were too big to carry, they cut them up in smaller pieces. How they pulled and pushed to get the pieces of wood to the water! They all had to pull together. Then, holding a piece firmly, they dived to the bottom to put it on the pile. The water-soaked logs from last night's work held the wood down.

Benjie was huffing and puffing as he

dragged a big piece of tree along the ground by himself. He heard a soft voice ask, "What are you doing with that tree? Why are you all cutting down trees?"

When Benjie heard those questions, he knew his rabbit friend, Cottontail, had come to see him. Cottontail always asked a lot of questions.

"Cottontail, how nice to see you!" cried Benjie. "I have so much to tell you. Sit here while I talk to you."

"Did you have a nice vacation?" asked Cottontail politely.

"Oh, we had the most fun and saw some of the most interesting animals," said Benjie. "Do you know that down South we saw a rabbit that could swim."

"Oh, no!" Cottontail looked shocked.

"Oh, yes it did," said Benjie knowingly. "It is called a marsh rabbit. And it was swimming in the water. What do you think of that?"

"Well, I think that would ruin his fur. I don't like to get wet at all. He surely must not be a handsome rabbit." Cottontail turned around to show off his furry, fluffy tail.

Benjie laughed at him. "He might think your life very dull without a swim," he said. "Then we saw a possum that hung by his tail from a tree and slept. He looked most uncomfortable, but he said he wasn't."

Cottontail looked interested. "Did you have any exciting things happen?" he asked.

"Yes," replied Benjie. "I saw a mink, and I thought it was an otter. I was just going to call out to him to be friendly when Father warned me. Minks like to eat young beavers! They hunt muskrats too, and nearly always get them.

Muskrats are smaller than we are, but they live much like we do."

Benjie liked explaining things, and his friend Cottontail was a good listener. "Then I met a tiny little animal called the shrew," he continued. "You can't imagine how tiny it was! And could it ever dig. He made a tunnel in the ground so fast I could hardly believe it. Have you ever seen a shrew around here?"

"Not that I can remember," replied Cottontail. "But I usually only look for food and then hurry home. I am not one for adventures. I am too timid and nervous."

Benjie's brother and sisters were busy working nearby. "Tell Cottontail about the wood pussy that shot you with her bomber," called his brother.

"Never mind that," said Benjie. He didn't like to remember how Mrs. Skunk had shot him with her stinky liquid gas.

"Oh, we have them around here," said Cottontail. "I have smelled them. Did you really get hit? I run the other way when I see a skunk."

"I will in the future," said Benjie. "I was glad I could go in the water and wash it off."

"Benjie!" called Father. "You are not getting the work done by talking all the time." Cottontail jumped at the sound of Father Beaver's big deep voice and hopped away.

"Come back again," called Benjie. "I didn't get to tell you why we are cutting down all these trees."

"Benjamin, this is serious business," said Father. "Every night gets cooler and that tells us cold weather is on the way. You must do your part to help. Mother and I are going to cut down trees further back. You kits will have to drag the branches to the pond. Now no more fooling around."

"I am sorry, Father," said Benjie.

Father and Mother cut trees a foot or more thick. They cut off the smaller branches and the kits took them to the feed pile. The big trunks were left to rot. This might seem wasteful, but the beavers are wise in the ways of the woods. They know that whenever they cut down a big tree, many small, tender sprouts will grow next spring. The new trees will make nice tender food close to the lodge for future needs.

Dangerous Flood Waters

Every day was about the same at the beaver pond. The beavers got up and worked all night to place wood on the feed pile for winter. Beavers sleep during the daytime and do their work and play at night. Many small animals work at night, so they will not be so easily seen and caught by the larger animals.

Benjie was proud as he saw the feed pile grow taller and taller. Surely they wouldn't go hungry this winter. But no one knows how long a winter will be, so the beavers kept on working.

One day rain began to fall and a fierce storm came up. Gusts of wind tore off the tops of trees. The beaver pond tossed with the largest waves Benjie had ever seen. The falling branches made it dangerous to work in the woods, so the family stayed in the warm, dry lodge. They would wait for better weather.

The rain poured down for three days. Father and Mother Beaver talked about how too much rain could damage their lodge. At last, Father said, "You kits stay here with your mother. I'm going out to see what the water is doing to our dam. I may be gone for awhile, but you stay right here inside the lodge."

Father was gone for many hours. Benjie and the other kits became very restless. It was nighttime and they should be outside working or playing.

Finally Mother said, "Come, kits, your Father is calling us. Maybe the rain has stopped!"

Everyone hurried out of the lodge and swam up to the surface of the water. The rain had not stopped. The kits would not have minded the rain, but their father seemed very upset. This was no time for young beavers to begin playing in the water.

"Come, everyone," Father called above the roar of the water. "The water is weakening our dam. We must get branches and sticks to make it stronger. All of you work as fast as you can!"

Benjie was frightened, but he knew he must work. He swam through the rough waters and got a branch and took it to the dam. He started to put it in place, but his father grabbed it from him, and put it where he wanted it. Quickly and one at a time he took the sticks from the others and placed them exactly where they were most needed. As soon as he would take a stick from a kit, he would command, "Go and get another. Hurry!"

Father worked from one end of the dam to the other, fitting in each branch carefully, and then grunted to the others to bring more.

The kits began to wonder if this gruff boss could be their gentle, loving father. He would not even let Mother put a branch on. Benjie realized that they were working to save their home and their winter supply of food.

All through the night the Beaver family worked together. The kits were so tired it seemed their little legs and jaws just could do no more. But their father urged them on. As dawn began to break Father decided that enough branches were in place. Now he ordered them to bring stones to weight down the new branches.

He allowed the kits to place the rocks on the dam themselves. The kits were half asleep as they worked. Benjie had never known he could get so tired.

Finally Father said they had done all they could to save the dam. Mother and the kits swam back home into the lodge and curled up to sleep. Father went back to the pile of branches he had made beside the dam earlier in the night. He would sleep on the pile so he would be close to what was happening.

Inside the lodge five very tired beavers were sleeping soundly. One of them stirred and woke up Benjie. He could hardly believe his sleepy eyes.

"Mother!" he cried. "Look! The water is coming right into our bedroom. Oh! Oh! Our whole house is flooded. Whatever shall we do?"

"Get out, kits! Swim out!" cried their mother. Once in the pond the four frightened beavers climbed up after her on top of their lodge. Only a little of the top of the lodge showed above the water.

Where was Father? Benjie looked all around him. Although it was near noon, the sky was dark, and the heavy rains continued to fall. Their stream had become a wide flowing river. Was that Father way down the stream?

"Look, Mother," exclaimed Benjie. "Isn't that Father way down the

stream?" Father was having a hard time swimming toward them against the rough water.

As Father drew near, Benjie called, "Oh, Father, our whole house is flooded. Whatever shall we do?"

The other kits began to whimper and cry. They huddled close to Mother. She looked at Father as if to also say, "What shall we do?"

Afloat on a Raft

With the rain pouring down, and the water in their pond flooding their home, Benjie was so frightened he didn't even think about eating.

Father looked at his family huddled on top of their lodge. He looked all around him. Then he said, "Come and follow me. The water is rough, but you are all strong swimmers. We are going to go across the pond to that high ridge over there."

At first the kits didn't want to go in the swift water. But when they saw Father and Mother swimming away, they dived in, too. How hard it was to keep from going down the stream. Benjie swam as hard as he could. They all climbed out of the water cold, hungry and still very tired from all their work on the dam.

"We must cut more branches and add them to this pile I have started," said Father. "Cut some brush, too, and weave it between the branches."

It was a mystery where they got their strength, but the Beaver family did not stop until the structure was nearly six feet high. Father cut down a young aspen tree for supper. The four miserable little kits huddled close to their mother and ate. Then they all climbed to the top of the brush pile and curled up close together. In spite of the heavy rain, they fell sound asleep.

The rain began to slow down toward evening, but the water was still rising in the pond. The Beaver family did not realize that the big man-made dam up the stream had broken. The broken dam had released so much water that it was flowing over much of the land. They were so tired they did not even wake up when the water crept up to their pile.

The waves splashed and the wind tugged at the branches. Suddenly the brush pile tore loose and swung out on the water. It was like a great raft being carried faster and faster along in the flood. Sometimes it got caught on a branch sticking out of the water. Then a sharp wave would come along and pull it free.

It was at one of the quick tugs that Benjie woke up. At first he did not realize what was happening. Where were they?

Father woke up and grunted in alarm. Then Mother and the others woke up.

When Benjie saw the swirling water all around them, he cried out, "Oh, Father, what has happened? We are moving along with the water!"

"Yes, I see," said Father. "The water must have pulled us into the stream. Be very careful and don't move around. This brush pile really wasn't made for floating. If you fall off, the stream will carry you away."

They all whimpered and clung tightly to their swirling brush pile. "I am glad Father had us make this pile good and strong," said Benjie.

"It is always important to do your work well," said Mother. She nuzzled each kit and assured them Father would do his best to care for them.

As they floated along they saw other creatures struggling in the water. "Oh, look at those frightened deer trying to get out of the water," said Benjie's brother.

"And there are some muskrats!" exclaimed Benjie. He called to them, "Come on, hang on to our raft." The muskrats clung to the branches and floated along with the beaver raft.

A squirrel was high in a tree chattering and scolding. He didn't seem to know what to do. "Guess the squirrel feels he should scold someone about all this," said Benjie. He was glad that his remark made his sisters giggle a little. It might help them not to be so frightened.

Benjie saw many other animals that had been driven from their homes along the stream. He wondered what had happened to his friend Cottontail.

"Oh, will we never stop?" cried Benjie. "I don't like to ride on this rough raft." No sooner had he spoken than the brush pile began to toss like a leaf. They had come to some rapids in the river. No one talked at all. They used all their strength to hold on as their raft tumbled through the roaring rapids.

At last they were in calmer water, and finally the rain stopped completely. They all sighed with relief.

"Let's cut a few branches from our pile and have a bite to eat," suggested Father. "But do not move around any more than you have to."

At least they could have something to eat, and they were so hungry. This bark didn't taste like the tender aspen trees, but it was better than nothing.

On Shore at Last

The Beaver family clung to the brush raft as it was carried downstream by the strong water. Father told Mother and the kits to go ahead and go to sleep. He would stay awake and watch out for danger. Although the rain had stopped the day was dark and cloudy. Mother and the kits dozed off in a short sleep once in a while.

Sometimes the pile would get caught on a branch from a tree that had fallen in the river. Then the Beaver family would just sit in the middle of the flood, sleepily watching the water rush by.

One time when the pile was caught, Father called, "Wake up, everybody. There is an island not too far away. Let's try to swim to it. Then we will be off of this rocking boat." But just as they were getting ready to dive into the water, the pile came loose and they were speeding down the river again.

"Hang on!" warned Mother.

"Oh, we are going faster than ever!" Benjie called out. "I am getting dizzy."

"Yes, it does seem we are moving very fast," answered Father in a worried voice.

"I hear a humming noise—like a lot of bees," said a sister as the pile jerked through some rapids.

They all listened, and as the humming got louder, they were suddenly sucked into another set of rapids. The beavers clung to each other in great fear as the brush pile spun around and around through the rough water.

Suddenly they were out of the rapids and their raft was swept clear across a broad new river. Just as they seemed about to reach the shore, a huge wave smashed into the raft and tore it apart.

All the beavers swam very hard against the swift water. "Help, help!" cried Benjie's sisters. "We just can't make it!"

Mother grabbed and held on to one of the sisters. Father grabbed the other. Benjie and his brother pretended they were having a wrestling match with the water and pushed and pushed themselves forward.

Finally they all crawled up on solid ground. They flopped down on the high bank of the river and rested for a long time. "I don't think I ever want to move again," sighed Benjie.

Now and then the beavers nuzzled each other, happy to be safe and all together. Mother inspected each kit to make sure they were all right.

At last Father grunted and got to his feet. "I think we had better go down this river bank a ways and see what is there," he said. Slowly the Beaver family crawled along the ground.

"The water is very calm here," said Mother. "Couldn't we swim along instead of walking? It would be much easier for us."

"Yes," said Father. "I think it is safe to go in the water here." They all followed as Father led the way downstream.

"I'm so tired," complained Benjie. "Can't we stop to get something to eat?"

"We'll look out for something, Benjie," said Father.

"Look!" cried Mother. "There is a willow grove. We could sleep in there, and have something to eat, too."

They all swam over to the willow grove. Father cut down a tender willow, and the hungry family quickly ate it up. It was not as sweet as the aspen bark, but the kits were so hungry they didn't care.

When their hunger was at last satisfied, the kits began to comb their fur and press the water from it. Father swam off in the water. Soon he came back with a nice surprise. He was proudly carrying the biggest lily root any of them had ever seen.

"Oh, Father," exclaimed Benjie, "what a lovely root! What a nice surprise!"

They all began to eat the delicious,

sweet dessert. When everyone had eaten plenty, Benjie gobbled up the last little bit.

"Now let's try to get some sleep," said Mother. Soon they were all curled together ready for the first really good sleep they had had in a long time.

Nothing disturbed them and they had been asleep for several hours when Benjie woke up suddenly. "Oh, my! Oh, Mother," he cried. "My tummy hurts so very much!"

Mother examined him and found him all puffed up. Soon the others were awake and crying with pain, too. Even Mother and Father did not feel too well. Benjie felt the worst of all. He had eaten the most and had eaten much too fast.

"What shall we do, Father?" asked Mother.

"I know what they need, but I do not know if I can find any around here," replied Father. "I will try, though."

Father left his sick family and made his way downstream looking along the shore for just the right medicine.

Good Medicine

Benjie and his family lay moaning in a willow grove. "I'll never eat too much again," cried Benjie.

"That will be the day!" said his sister. Then she held her tummy and rolled over with the pain.

"It was the kind of food we ate," said Mother. "Father has gone to find some medicine for us. I hope it doesn't take him too long."

Father Beaver swam downstream and sniffed the air. His nose would tell him when he found the right tree that would help his family. He noticed a bright light coming up along the shore. Then he heard a loud thundering noise that sounded like the roar of the flood. From the other direction came another light, and when it met the first, a long, shrill whistle sounded in the night. Father thwacked his tail, and dived to the river bottom. Cautiously he came up. Two trains rumbled on, and Father finally saw that these two noisy monsters would do him no harm.

Once again he held his head up high and sniffed the air. He smelled people, and saw twinkling lights of houses. Then he began to smell the scent of the bark he was looking for. Closer and closer he swam to the smell until he was at the very place where the tree grew. As he drew near the bank, he saw the tree was in a place that was guarded by a barking dog. The dog rushed to the edge of the water and barked and barked.

Soon the door of a house opened and people came out. They flashed a bright light on the river and caught a glimpse of Father Beaver.

"Look, look!" the man cried. "It is a

beaver. Come, let's go watch him."

But Father didn't want to be watched. He dived to the bottom of the river and stayed there. Finally the people gave up and went back into the house, taking the dog with them.

Father made sure all was safe, then crawled upon the bank, and cut off a low branch of a red cedar tree. He quickly swam back to his family with it.

"Eat this bark and the evergreen leaves, and you will soon feel better," commanded Father. "This is just the medicine you need."

They all obediently started to eat the leaves he had brought them.

"Did you have trouble finding this medicine?" asked Benjie, who was already feeling better.

"I did have some excitement on the way," admitted Father. "I saw two huge monsters with bright lights and loud noises. But they did not hurt me," said Father.

"Oh, my!" exclaimed Benjie. "What kind of animals were they?"

Father laughed. "They were not animals," he said. "They were man-made things that travel. Maybe you will see one someday."

"I don't think I want to," said Benjie.

"But I did meet a barking animal that did not want to let me get this branch," Father told them. "I had to wait a long time for him to go away."

"Do you think we are ready to travel?" asked Mother.

Father looked at each one. "How do you kits feel?"

"Almost as good as ever," answered Benjie.

"Fine! Then let's be on our way," replied Father. "We must find a place to live and get a home built. We must gather enough food for the winter."

"Do not worry, Father," assured Benjie. "We will help you. I won't play one little bit. I will just work and work."

"Sure, until you start to play," laughed his brother.

"Don't tease Benjie," scolded Mother. "He means to work, but the play just comes out in him all the time."

"How about a little game of tag as we swim down the river?" suggested Benjie.

"See what I mean?" said his brother. He began to chase Benjie, who was already on his way.

Journey's End

The Beaver family swam for two nights downstream in the wide river. They had passed under many bridges and swam past many islands. Occasionally they stopped off for a rest and to press the water from their fur. They certainly were very careful what they ate. They did not want to get sick again.

The third evening the beavers came to a river valley. The river divided into many channels, ponds and inlets, and wandered in among marshes and a brush-covered island. Cottonwood and maple trees grew in the thick woods. Aspen trees could be seen on the higher ground. Pond lilies and other plants beavers love to eat were growing in great clusters. Father knew he had found their new home.

Father led his family into a marshy place. A large swamp maple had fallen across the water. Under the tree's great roots was a roomy cave. It was large enough for them to sleep in until they could make a new lodge.

"Oh, I like it here!" Benjie cried happily. "What a lot of water and so many things to see."

"Well, right now we are thinking about a place to sleep," said Mother.

Father swam into the cave and began to dig eagerly. He wanted to make the room a little larger. Sand began to fly as he dug.

"Hey, you are throwing sand in our eyes," cried Benjie's brother.

"I'm sorry," said Father. "You'd better move away as I want to make our apartment bigger."

When they saw the nice comfortable

den Father had made they quickly forgave him. They had a hearty supper of cottonwood bark, and soon crawled into the bed. The kits curled up near each other and were soon asleep.

Mother and Father did not go to bed yet. They stayed up and explored all the area. The first thing they would need was a deep pond. They found one not far away. They agreed to start building here.

"Look at that huge, hollow elm tree on the bank," said Father. "I am going to use this as part of our family's new lodge."

"But how?" asked Mother. "It is not in the water."

"We will dig through the bank to the tree," explained Father. "The roots will be part of our roof. We will build the lodge partly in the water and partly on the bank. Then we'll make the tunnels under the water up into the lodge. That way we will still be safe from enemy animals."

Mother got very excited as she understood Father's plan. It would be a wonderful lodge. The hollow tree would let fresh air into their lodge.

Of course, beavers must always have air in their homes. They have no outside doors or windows. But at the very tip of the lodge they leave a tiny hole. On very cold days steam made by the beavers' breath can be seen coming out of the hole in the lodge. Also air bubbles come in with them as the beavers come into the lodge. The bubbles cling to their fur and help give the beavers enough air to breathe.

"Let's start building right away," said Mother. "We could surprise the kits."

Father didn't agree. "No, we had better rest. It will be surprise enough for them to see the place. Besides, it will be nicer if we all build together."

"You are right," answered Mother. "I am very tired. We'd better go back to the kits and sleep. I don't want them to wake up and find us gone. They might become frightened."

"They certainly were brave through all that trouble," said Father proudly. "Even Benjie obeyed and did what he was told."

"Yes," said Mother fondly. "He is going to grow up to be a fine beaver like his Father."

A New Home

Benjie awoke, stretched and yawned. "Why, where am I?" For a minute he forgot where he was. Then he remembered the flood that had destroyed his home and carried them far away. He looked over and saw Mother and Father still sleeping in the one room apartment under the tree. He wanted to go out for a swim, but thought he had better wait for the rest of the family.

"Oh, well, I could always sharpen my teeth on one of these roots. I haven't had a good chew in a long time," said Benjie. With that he began to gnaw on one of the large roots of the tree. Beavers' teeth grow all the time, and they have to keep using them to wear them off and keep them sharp. If they get too long, they cannot use them. But when a beaver chops and gnaws it makes a lot of noise and Benjie was making a lot of noise chopping away at the root. It was not long until the rest of the Beaver family was awake.

"What a noisy beaver!" exclaimed

Mother. "Does that root taste good?"

"Oh, I am not eating it. I am just sharpening my teeth," replied Benjie. "Good morning, everyone. When can we go for a swim?"

"Right away," said Father. "And Benjie, you certainly will need sharp teeth. We have a lot of work to do."

"Oh, goodie," cried all the kits. Oh, how they did love to work!

"Come," said Mother, "we will show you where we are going to build our new home." They all swam out into the water and toward the pond Father and Mother had found. They showed the hollow elm to the kits and explained what they were going to do.

"And we must start right away. Winter is very close and soon ice will cover our pond," said Father.

Father dived to the bottom of the pool near the bank. He started to tunnel a runway upward and back into the bank, straight toward the hollow elm. This was very hard digging because the ground was made of clay and hardpan. Father did not mind this hard work. The runways would be strong and would not cave in when they swam in and out.

They would not have to worry about the sandy surface soil falling in.

Mother hollowed out several spacious rooms under the roof of the elm roots. She was delighted with the lovely new house they were going to have. She made a large dining room, and several bedrooms.

The kits were busy gathering sticks, stones and mud to cover up the runways and to build up the lodge around the base of the tree. It was necessary to have a strong, deep cover to protect the underground lodge. The kits knew just how to lay the sticks. They would dive to the bottom of the pond to get mud. They put the mud on the sticks to hold them together. They added stones on top of the sticks and mud. They were really very clever builders. Each time they brought up mud and stones, they were making their pond deeper.

Benjie always swam a little ways from the new home when he got mud or stones, hoping he would see something new. He was so anxious to explore the whole river valley, but he knew that right now they all had to work.

He dived down for some mud, and

when he came up he saw a group of ducks not far away. They were eating and the only sound he could hear was soft "quack-quacks" as they dipped their bills into the water. Still holding his mud, Benjie swam quietly toward them. Although Benjie thought he was not making a sound, the ducks were quick to realize something was coming.

With a great whirring of wings, they all arose from the water at once and flew away.

The sudden sound and motion surprised Benjie. He threw the mud up in the air and dived to the bottom of the pond. He stayed down for a while, and then he thought how silly he was to be frightened by some ducks. Slowly he came up and looked around. All was quiet again. He swam back to the other beavers.

"Where is the mud you went to get?" asked his brother. "I need it right here."

"I lost it," said Benjie.

"Lost it! Now how can you lose mud?" asked his brother.

"Well, it wasn't easy," replied Benjie. "Oh, never mind. I'll go get some more." He didn't want to tell his brother the ducks had frightened him and made him drop the mud.

"If you don't find the same handful, I'll take any old mud you find," teased his brother.

"Very funny," remarked Benjie, and he gave his brother a push as he dived to the bottom of the water again.

A Feed Pile
for Winter

Each evening as the Beaver family awoke the air was crisper and the water colder. This made them work even harder, for they knew that soon the very cold winter would arrive. Finally the day came when the lodge was finished. The pile around the elm tree was nearly twenty feet across and ten feet high. Then they covered the runways from the tree to the water with a six-foot covering.

Father dug two more runways into the lodge. A beaver's home always has many entrances. If they hear an enemy coming, they can all swim safely up the waterways into their lodge.

"I am going to dig a den on the other side of the pond just in case of an emergency," said Father. "It is always good to have another place of safety. Then we must start on a new feed pile for winter."

"That is a job I really like," said Benjie.

"Yes, we know," said his sister, "because you can snack all the time."

"You kits go and look for trees that are still green with leaves that are fresh. There are many good trees growing along this pond," said Mother.

In no time at all the young beavers were gnawing away at the tender young trees. They knew it would take many trees and branches to keep them through the winter.

"It's too bad our feed pile didn't float down with us," said Benjie.

"It probably was scattered all over," said his brother. "I am just glad we were not scattered. At least we are all together and have a nice new home."

"Benjie," called his father. "I want all of you to come over here."

The beavers hurried to Father as fast as their short legs would take them. He was standing by a large cottonwood tree that was growing about 60 feet back from the bank of the pond.

"We are going to cut down this big tree and it will fall in the pond. It will be the beginning of our feed pile," explained Father. "But the tree is very big around, and I need all of you to help."

They all began to work. First they gnawed a wide band around the trunk of the tree. Then, chip by chip, they cut a thin wedge with their chisel teeth until the trunk snapped. Father smacked his tail on the ground to warn that the tree was ready to fall. The beavers scurried out of the way. Father had figured just right, and the top of the leafy tree landed in the water right where he had planned.

"Good work!" cheered all the beavers. How proud they were of their clever Father.

"Now we will place other branches on the floating end of the tree. The weight of the green wood will sink the pile deeper and deeper," explained Father.

For many days the beavers did nothing but cut wood for the feed pile. They worked all around the pond, cutting the fresh green trees. Benjie noticed a trail on the bank opposite their lodge. He wondered who made it and who walked on it. It was not long until he found out. He saw some beautiful white-tailed deer passing by in the twilight.

He decided to follow them down the path a ways to see what they did. He

noticed one handsome buck rubbing his
horns on an elm tree.

"Now, why does he want to do that?"
wondered Benjie. He saw the buck
charge the small tree and intertwine its
branches between his horns. How he did
wrestle with it!

Benjie hurried back to his family.
"Come and watch a buck fight with a
tree. What does it mean?"

"Benjie, you do find the queerest
things," said Mother.

"Father, you must know what it
means. Will you tell us?" asked Benjie.

Father laughed. "First we'll watch a while and then I will explain it to you," he said. "It is really a love story."

"Oh, you are joking," cried Benjie.

"You wait and see," said Father mysteriously.

The Fighting Bucks

The Beaver family all hurried down the deer trail to watch a big buck wrestle with a tree.

"Father, what do you mean this is a love story?" asked Benjie. "Is the deer in love with the tree?"

"Of course not." Father laughed and all the others laughed, too.

"Well, I just don't understand it," said Benjie, a bit insulted that his whole family would laugh at him.

"This is the time of the year that the man deer looks for a lady deer to come and live with him. It is called the mating season. The man deer, or buck, often has to fight another buck in order to get a lady deer, or doe as she is called. This buck is really practicing," explained Father.

"Oh, you mean he is pretending that the tree is another deer with horns," said Benjie.

"That is right," said Father. "Let's watch him in his training." As the beavers watched, the deer charged the young tree and intertwined its branches between his horns. Soon the deer was so closely interwoven with the tree that he seemed fastened to it.

"Now he will never get free," said Benjie's sister.

"Just watch," answered Father.

The deer kneeled to the ground and heaved. You could see his neck swelling with effort. Then with a great grunt he pulled his antlers free.

"My, how strong he really is," whispered Benjie. "Are deers friendly with beavers?"

"They won't bother us," answered Mother. "And of course we wouldn't want to frighten them."

"Do beavers ever have to fight for a mate?" asked Benjie's sister.

"Sometimes," said Father, "but once we find the right mate we live together the rest of our lives." He gave Mother a tender nuzzle. Mother looked very pleased and gave a grunt of pleasure.

"Did you fight for Mother?" asked Benjie, who hoped there had been a big battle and Father had won.

"No, I am afraid not," said Father. "When I found your mother, she was walking alone. I knew I wanted her for my mate as soon as I saw her. Now I not only have a wonderful mate, but four beaver children!"

"Oh, Father," cried Benjie, "you are the best father ever. I want to be a good father like you when I grow up."

"Look," whispered Mother as she pointed at the trail. The beavers saw a handsome six-point buck coming down the trail with a beautiful doe. They had not come far when the other buck that had been wrestling with the tree saw them. He stared at the beautiful lady deer and wanted her for his mate. He challenged the other buck to a fight.

The two bucks stamped and pawed the ground. Then they lowered their heads and charged each other. The crash of their horns rang through the woods.

"Oh, my!" cried Benjie. "Look at them fight!"

Again and again the bucks charged and clashed their heads together. Each was trying to put his sharp horns in the other's flank or stomach. They leaped and turned gracefully, always facing each other to charge again. Over and over their horns clashed in a fierce

contest to see who could force the other
to give way.

"I don't want the kits to watch this
anymore," said Mother. "I don't feel
safe. I am going to take them home."

"That is a good idea," said Father.

"But I want to see what happens,"
begged Benjie.

"I will watch from a safe place," said
Father, "and I promise to tell you what
happens."

"All right," said Benjie. He was
disappointed but he knew Father would
keep his promise. Mother and the four
kits swam back to the lodge.

"Go to sleep now," said Mother.
"Father will tell us all about the battle
tomorrow."

Love Story with a Sad Ending

Father had gone as far away from the fighting deer as he could and yet watch the battle. The crashes and thuds continued. He was watching because he promised to tell his family about it, but he also was watching to make sure this struggle didn't threaten his family and home.

As the two bucks struggled on, the pretty doe wandered off into the woods. Other deer that came along the trail stopped to watch the battle.

It was really beginning to get quite light, and Father was getting worried. He did not want to stay out in the bright light of the day, and yet he wanted to see the end of the battle.

By now the bucks had pushed until they were very near the pond. One tried to pull away from the other, but their horns were locked together. They could not get apart. They both became more and more angry as they tried to pull apart. Then one gave a mighty shove and they fell into the water. Father quickly swam over by the lodge and was ready to dive in if any danger seemed to threaten him.

Father saw the pretty doe going down the trail with another buck. But by now the two that were fighting probably were not thinking of the lady deer. They were struggling to free themselves of each other. They struggled desperately in the water, blowing the water out of their nostrils.

One buck pushed the other into deep water and held him under. The poor buck drowned. Now that there was no one to fight against, the other deer dragged himself and the drowned deer upon the bank. He was still locked to the dead deer.

He worked very hard to free himself, but he could not. He fell back so tired that he just lay down with his burden, breathing heavily.

"I must go in," thought Father. "It is just too light for safety." He went into the lodge and found the others all asleep. He pressed some of the water out of his fur, and was soon fast asleep.

It seemed he had just shut his eyes

when four eager beavers were crawling all over him. They pulled his fur and sat on his tail.

"Is this any way to wake up a father?" exclaimed Father. He gave his tail a quick pull and Benjie fell off. The others tumbled down, too.

"Tell us about the fight," they all cried.

"Very well, I will," replied Father. So he told them all that happened, and they "oh'ed" and "ah'ed" all the way through the exciting story.

"What a shame to fight like that," said Benjie's sister.

"And to think the lady deer didn't even wait for one of them to win," said Mother.

"That is the way it is with women," said Father with a twinkle in his eye. "They change their minds."

"Not always," replied Mother rather sharply.

"Father is only teasing," said Benjie. "He knows you are the best mother and mate in the world. I wonder what happened to the live deer."

"Well, the battle is over, and nothing was won really. It was a love story with a very sad ending," said Mother.

"Let's swim out and get some more trees for the feed pile," suggested Father. "I want to make sure we have enough for the winter." Soon the beavers were out in the pond splashing, and taking their bath. They swam over to the bank to climb up to begin to cut trees.

"Did you hear something move?" whispered Mother to Father.

"Yes," said Father. "Stay here with the kits in the water. I will go downstream to see what it is."

Father was very surprised to find the deer still struggling to be free of the dead

deer. He had dragged it down the bank of the pond a short way. The deer could do nothing but die of starvation now. How sad.

Some scent in the air made Father quickly look the other way. He saw a large bobcat creeping along the trail toward the trapped buck on the bank. He watched in horror as the bobcat leaped through the air and landed on the dead deer. When the living buck saw his enemy, he twisted his head with one last bit of strength and broke the prong of the antler that was holding him. Before the wildcat could leap again, the deer had bounded away to safety.

The bobcat turned and seemed to stare right at Father. Father thwacked his tail in danger and they all swam for the lodge. They were so afraid the bobcat might still be around that they stayed inside for a long, long while.

"I am so glad the deer got free," said Benjie. "Maybe he will find another mate."

"I hope he doesn't have such a hard time with the next one," said Mother.

Benjie's Secret Hiding Place

The Beaver family stayed in their lodge for almost two nights and two days. At last Father swam out of the lodge and explored all around for any signs of danger. All was quiet and peaceful on the pond. He called the others out.

Father told his family, "We still have some work to do on our feed pile."

Mother said, "We certainly have had a lot of exciting interruptions."

"I still want to explore all around here," added Benjie.

"You will have plenty of time later," Father replied. "We are going to be here for a long time."

"Right now we must get our feed pile finished," answered Mother.

They all went to work and nothing unusual happened for several nights. By the time the ice began to cover the pond, the pile of nice tender branches was 15 feet across and sunk deep into the water.

This would surely be more than enough to keep the beavers fed, even if the winter was long and hard.

They were snug and warm in their well-built home and they didn't care if it was bitter cold and often snowing outside. Mother and Father took long naps. They enjoyed this rest after the hard work they had done to get the lodge built and the feed pile ready.

Benjie, his brother and sisters slept more than in the summer. But young busy beavers could not be expected to sleep as much as Mother and Father. They had no trouble keeping busy or having fun.

"Let's play hide-and-seek," said Benjie. "We have a lot of rooms and runways. I'll hide first and you see if you can find me."

"Oh, that won't be hard," the others said. "We know every room in this lodge, and the runways too. No fair going into Mother and Father's room as they are sleeping."

What a great time they had with this game, and they would squeal with delight when they found the one that was hiding. Then Benjie had a good idea. He thought of a place to hide that no one could find.

"My turn to hide again," called Benjie. "Everybody close your eyes."

"Don't be silly," said his sister. "It is so dark in here we can't see much anyway. Besides you know we do not have strong eyes. We find you by listening and smelling."

"Just make sure you wait long enough," Benjie said excitedly. He swam in the waterway to fool the others. Then he crawled back into the lodge and climbed up into the trunk of the hollow elm tree around which the lodge was built. "Now they will never find me," Benjie thought happily.

The others looked and looked and each time they met back in their room, there was no Benjie to be found.

"Now where could he go?" asked his brother.

"You don't suppose he went out of the lodge into the pool, do you?" asked his sister.

"Oh, no, he wouldn't do that. He knows he can't go out alone in this cold winter weather," said his brother.

"Let's look again," they said. So off they went to make the rounds of the rooms and the waterways. But no Benjie!

"I am worried," said his sister. "Let's tell Father and Mother. Maybe he is in trouble."

They hurried to their parents' room and told them about the missing Benjie. "Are you sure you looked everywhere?" asked Father.

"Oh, yes, we looked everywhere twice," they said.

"But you didn't look in the right place or you would have found him," said Father mysteriously.

"Do you know where he is?" they asked.

Father chuckled. "Yes, I think I do. But I am not going to give his secret away. He might want to use it again. I know how we can get him to come out of his hiding place though."

"How?" they all cried.

"Just watch and see," replied Father. Father swam out of the lodge and dived into the chilly water under the ice. He brought in a nice juicy branch for breakfast.

Soon the beavers were chopping away on the food and making a lot of noise, as beavers do when they eat. Beavers have good ears, and Benjie could hear them all eating from where he was hiding. He could not stay away. His tummy just had to have some of that good food. He climbed down out of his hiding spot and made his way into the dining room of the lodge.

"Why, look who is here," said Father. He tried to look surprised, but there was a smile on his face.

"Where were you, Benjie?" called the other kits.

"That's for me to know and for you to find out," replied Benjie.

The Muskrat Family

Benjie's sisters and brother were rather upset that he wouldn't tell them his secret hiding place.

"You will find it someday," said Benjie. "But until then, I am going to keep it a secret."

Benjie's brother had a good idea. "Let's have a woodcutting contest. We need to sharpen our teeth. Father brought in a big branch. We can cut it into four pieces, and then shred it up fine for our beds. Then they will be nice and soft to sleep on."

They all agreed this would be a fun way to get some work done. The chips soon were flying, and, oh, the noise they made! Benjie kept stopping to say, "I am winning. I know I am." Mother and Father came in to watch.

"I didn't know we had such hard working children," said Father. "We'll have to give them more work to do in the spring."

"Why, yes," agreed Mother with a teasing smile. "You and I won't have to do a thing."

"You are teasing us," said Benjie. He knew it was all in fun. "See, I am winning." But Benjie stopped to talk so much that he didn't win after all. His quiet, hard working sister was finished first.

Mother and Father clapped for all of them and helped them spread the chips around on their beds.

"Now go take a dip in the waterway. It will make you feel nice and clean," said Mother. They all swam away in a different waterway. Benjie went into the extra tunnel that Father had made in case of an emergency. They did not use it too often. Benjie was splashing away, when he heard a sound behind him. He turned around and there to his surprise were thirteen muskrats!

"Hello," said the father muskrat in a friendly way. "I wonder if we could build a nest in the side of this tunnel for the winter? We would be good neighbors."

"I really couldn't say," replied Benjie in surprise. "I am only a kit. My father would have to give you permission. I will go call him."

Benjie quickly swam back to his

parents. "Father, Mother, come see what I have found in the runway!" Then he couldn't wait for them to see and rushed on to say, "Thirteen muskrats!"

"Benjie, are you sure you saw thirteen muskrats?" asked his mother in a rather cross voice. She didn't want Benjie making up stories.

"Honest, Mother, and they want to live with us—or at least in the waterway," replied Benjie.

"Well, we had better go see about this," said Father. Benjie led the way and, sure enough, the muskrat family was waiting for them. Benjie looked them all over as Father talked to them. The father muskrat was only half the size of Benjie. His rat-like tail seemed very small. Benjie looked back at his own broad paddle tail. He was glad his tail was just like it should be for beavers.

Father and Mother agreed to let the Muskrat family build a nest in the waterway. But they must not bother the Beaver family or come into the lodge. The Muskrat family promised that they would not, and that they had their own food supply.

So it was that a muskrat family came

to live in the waterway of the beaver lodge. Benjie and the other kits often went to visit and watch them. In a way, they were like the Beaver family, yet they were different enough to make Benjie curious.

He had met one muskrat on his vacation last summer, but he didn't really have a chance to get acquainted.

"What do you like to eat?" he asked one of the little muskrats.

"We have a whole winter's supply of deer-tongue potatoes. We like to eat them," the little muskrat replied. "Of course we like clams, too."

"What is a deer-tongue potato?" asked Benjie.

"It is a root plant. It is very delicious. The next time my father brings some in, I will let you taste one," he promised.

"Thank you," said Benjie. But he wondered if he should. He remembered the tummy ache he had once from eating the wrong kind of food. Maybe the little muskrat would forget his promise and there was no need to worry about it now.

The Muskrat family was pleasant all right, but the young ones didn't want to play with the beaver kits. Maybe they thought the beavers were too big and eager. At first Benjie was hurt because of this. But soon the two families became accustomed to living in the same place. They did not bother each other too much and both families lived their own lives. The beaver kits went back to their own games and had a good time together.

The Waiting Animal

Benjie and his family snuggled together in their new home because it was cold outside. Father and Mother enjoyed the rest they were getting now. They took long naps in their bedroom. Father would go out once in a while and bring in a piece of wood from their food supply. Then they would all have a good time eating.

"Ho, hum," said Benjie. "I just can't sleep all the time. I wish I had something exciting to do. I surely miss being able to go out in the pond and perform my water tricks."

"The water would be very cold now," reminded his sister. "Besides, Father says we cannot go out until he tells us it is safe."

"The pond is all covered with ice," added his brother. "You would just bump your head on the ice anyway. Then we could call you blockhead!"

"Very funny!" replied Benjie. "I can see you are not going to give me any good ideas of things to do. I think I will swim down one of the tunnels and see how the muskrat family is doing."

Benjie was swimming down the tunnelway to get to the muskrats' little home when he heard a different kind of noise. He smelled a different scent, too. It was not a beaver scent or a muskrat scent. He stopped. He was very quiet.

As he looked carefully, he soon saw a large animal swimming in the waterway. It was going toward the muskrats' home. The animal was a mink, and he was looking for food. A muskrat dinner would suit him just fine.

Just then the muskrats saw what was coming. They squealed and swam away as fast as they could out into the cold pond waters. Benjie quickly turned around and swam back to the lodge. He was all excited and out of breath.

"Now what terrible thing has happened?" asked his brother.

"A mink, a big, black mink is after the muskrat family!" exclaimed Benjie. "They swam away, but the mink might come after us."

One of his sisters quickly said, "Let's go tell Father. He will know what to do." The four young beavers soon were gathered around Father and Mother. Benjie told them about the mink and the muskrats.

"Well, I do not think we have to worry too much," said Father. "I am sure the muskrats got away, and I don't think that mink will come after us. We are much too big for him. I will swim down to see what is happening. All of you wait here."

"I want to go too," begged Benjie. "I was big enough to find him. Why can't I go?"

"No," said Mother. "Remember you

didn't go out to find a mink. It was just an accident that you found it. Father will go and see what is happening."

Father swam down the tunnelway very quietly. Beavers can swim making hardly a noise or ripple in the water. Soon he swam back to his family and told them that they were safe.

"That mink will have a long wait," he said, "because the muskrat family will not come back. It will be a good joke on him. He will get mighty hungry, too!"

"You mean the family will never come back to live with us?" asked Benjie. "Even if they weren't too friendly, I will miss them. It was nice to know someone else was around if you wanted to visit."

"No, they won't come back to a place of danger," answered Father. "But maybe you will see them again when the weather gets warmer and we can go out in the water again. But for now I want you all to stay in your room. We won't pester that old mink. Just let him sit and wait."

"Come on," said Benjie. "Let's go play tag in our room while we wait for the mink to wait."

Father's Funny Mistake

The game of tag in their bedroom didn't turn out to be such fun after all. The room was not very large, and they kept messing up their chip bed. Besides, beavers cannot move fast on the ground, so it turned out to be a pretty slow game of tag.

"Oh, dear," sighed Benjie, "this isn't my idea of fun at all. I wonder if that mink is still out in the tunnel. He didn't look so dangerous to me. Just because those silly muskrats were afraid of him, I'm not."

"You can talk brave because you are safe in your room," said his brother, "but I noticed you surely came running back fast after you first saw him."

"Yes," said his sister, "and don't forget he came in to eat the muskrats. You would run too if someone came to eat you."

"Who would want to eat Benjie?" added his sister. "He is too tough!"

"I'm not that tough!" answered Benjie. "I would be good to eat, if I wanted to be eaten. Not that I would ever want to be eaten, but I know I would be delicious!"

Mother poked her head into the room. "My, this sounds like a very interesting discussion. Who is going to eat whom and why?"

The young beavers all laughed and gathered around Mother.

"Is the mink still out there?" asked Benjie.

"Yes, he is," replied Mother. "I have come to tell you not to go out into the waterways. Father wants you to stay here in the lodge. He has gone out another tunnel to bring in some food, then you can come down into the dining room."

When beavers make a home, they make a big room in which to eat. They don't have table and chairs as people do, but they like to have a special room for eating. Then they clean up all the scraps and carry them out into the water to float away. They like a neat place in which to live. They make other little rooms to sleep in, and chop up wood to make soft beds.

Mother and Father Beaver slept in one room, and the young beavers had another room. The kits all slept close together on one bed of chips. Father had made many tunnels leading out of the lodge, so they could leave quickly or come in quickly when there was danger.

"Mother, please tell us some things that happened while we were babies," begged Benjie.

"Yes," cried all the others. "Tell us something about our family."

The young beavers never got tired of listening to Mother tell about their family. They liked to hear her tell how she and Father had worked together to make a lodge when the kits were just tiny babies.

"Now, let's see. What could I tell you today?" wondered Mother. "Oh, I know. I will tell you about the lodge Father built for us. You see, we didn't have a home when you were born. It had been washed away. And so were Father and our older kits. I thought I was left all alone. When you were born you had to live in a den, a hole dug in the side of the bank of the stream. You were so tiny! None of you was big enough to help with the work at all. I didn't know what I was going to do."

"I'll bet I wanted to help," said Benjie.

"Maybe you did, but you couldn't, you funny fellow," laughed Mother.

"Stop interrupting, Benjie," scolded his sister. "We want to hear."

"Then there was Father swimming near that den!" continued Mother. "I was so happy to see that big, handsome beaver!"

"Oh, yes," agreed all the kits. "Father is a big, handsome beaver!"

Mother happily nuzzled each beaver kit until they all felt her love for them.

"Then," continued Benjie at last, "that big, handsome beaver built you and us a nice new home—didn't he?"

"Yes, he did," agreed Mother with a happy grunt. "How hard he worked to build that lodge! It was so beautiful. I helped him by felling trees and bringing in branches. But he did most of the work. Finally he took me to the lodge. It was finished! We swam underwater to one of the waterways leading to the lodge. But Father had been so busy and was so excited about making the new home for us that he forgot to hollow out any rooms! He was so embarrassed. But I helped him and soon we had three nice rooms just like we have in this house. Then we moved you from that den into your first real home."

The young beavers all laughed over Father's funny mistake. "That sounds like a Benjie trick," teased his brother. They laughed even harder, and Father came in to see what was so funny. They ran over to him and hugged him, and said, "You are a funny Father."

"Have you been telling stories about me again?" Father asked Mother.

Mother gave Father a big beaver smile and said, "What do you think?"

Unwelcome Visitors

"Does anyone want anything to eat in this family?" called Father. "I brought in some food for a snack."

All the beavers hurried to the dining room. It seemed as though they were always hungry. Especially the young beavers. And especially Benjie! He was the first one to reach the dining room.

But Benjie waited for the others to arrive and soon they were all chopping away with their strong orange-colored teeth and enjoying a good meal.

"When can I go out to the feed pile with you, Father?" asked Benjie.

"You kits have been very good about staying in and as soon as that mink leaves us, I'll take you out for a little while," promised Father.

"Oh, goody. Why don't you just go tell that mink to leave?" suggested Benjie's brother.

"I hardly think that would be the thing to do," replied Father. "Don't worry, he will get hungry and be tired of waiting pretty soon."

And the old mink was getting tired. In fact he was dozing in the top of the waterway waiting for the muskrats to return home. Half asleep and half awake, he suddenly crouched ready to kill. To his great surprise there appeared a big, sleek otter at the entrance of the tunnel. The frightened mink turned and dashed up the waterway right into the beaver's dining room. He ran by the startled Beaver family and sprang up through the opening into the hollow elm tree. And he was gone!

"What was all that about?" cried Mother.

"Something must be after him," said Father. And before they could say another word in came an entire otter family ... mother, father and three noisy otter cubs.

The otters seemed to want to be friendly. They went right up to Father and Mother and tried to make friends. The young otters ran all over the place trying to get the beavers to play with them.

The Beaver family was very surprised at this visit. Father and Mother humped their backs and hissed at the otters.

When the mother otter heard this sound, she knew they were not welcome. She called her cubs and they all swam merrily out the tunnel and went on their way through the icy water.

"My, but we had some rude visitors," exclaimed Mother. "I hope you kits never act like that. Did you ever see such noisy children?"

"They surely did move fast," said Benjie. "They could play tag without any trouble at all!" He was really wishing they could have stayed and played awhile. "Maybe we will all meet again sometime," he added, always wanting to make new friends.

"I guess that mink is gone for good," Father said, very amused. "I would like to have seen the surprised look on his face when old man otter came in instead of the muskrats."

"That was a good joke on him," laughed the others. "But he did give us a scare as he ran through the room."

"Now we can go out in the water?" asked Benjie.

"Not tonight, Benjie," answered Father. "We have had enough excitement for today."

"Right now you can help me carry the scraps out to the waterway," said Mother.

The young beavers helped Mother carry the scraps away and clean up the room. Then they all sat and combed their fur. They pressed the water out and combed and combed with their long claws. How thick and long their fur had grown.

"You all look so nice and clean," said Mother, as she admired her children. "Now off to bed with you." The kits all gave Mother a hug and went tumbling into their bed.

Bubbles Under Ice

Benjie was the first to awaken from the long winter day's nap. Even though he could not see out of his home, he knew that the sun had gone down and it was dark outside. Beavers sleep during the day and go out at night. They have learned to do their work in the dark, and love the cool dark nights.

Benjie stretched and gave a beaver grunt. Perhaps tonight Father would take them out of the lodge. He and his sisters and his brother had been allowed to play in the waterways and get wet, but they could not go all the way out into the pond. Only Father had gone out to get food. Even Mother seemed content to stay inside and rest.

"Wake up, everyone," called Benjie. "It is time to get up and eat and go out into the water." Slowly the other beaver kits began to wake up. After stretching and yawning they went into Mother's and Father's bedroom. They tugged Father to wake him up.

"What is all the hurry?" Father asked

as he yawned.

"We are so hungry," answered Benjie.

"Well, then go on out and get a piece of wood from the pile," said Father, as he snuggled down in his bed.

"All by ourselves?" asked Benjie. "Aren't you going to come with us?"

"What's the matter? Don't you remember where we put the wood?" asked Father.

"Well, sure I do. All the times we dived to the bottom of the pond to put the wood there . . . it must have been a million times!" replied Benjie.

"I hardly think a million," laughed Mother, "or the whole pond would be full of wood and we would have no place to stay."

"I want to go out in the water, but I don't care to go alone for the first time," said Benjie.

"We thought you were so brave," said his sisters.

"I am brave! I just don't want to be brave alone!" replied Benjie.

"Benjie is right," said Father. "I was only teasing you. I will go out first and scout around. I don't think there is any danger, but it is better to be sure than sorry. You wait here."

Father dived out of the lodge into the icy water. He swam all around the lodge and the woodpile. He sniffed for enemies, and could smell none. Soon he was back in the lodge calling for the young beavers to follow him.

Benjie was the first to dive after Father into the cold water. Brrrr, what cold water, thought Benjie. He could feel it clear through his thick fur.

The other beavers followed and they each did a few swimming tricks in the water. As they swam, the air they gradually exhaled rose in large bubbles through the water and clung to the underside of the ice that covered the pond. Wherever they swam, they left a ribbon of bubbles.

Beavers can stay underwater as long as ten minutes, but they didn't even want to try it in the cold water. Soon they were back in the lodge taking deep breaths of warm air. Father followed after them. "What, so tired of the water already? I thought you wanted to go out to play."

"There isn't much you can do out there," replied Benjie. "We have to come in for breaths of air. If we go to the top of the water, we bump into the hard ice. When will it ever melt, so we can breathe fresh air again?" asked Benjie.

"Well, not for some time yet. We have a lot of cold weather ahead of us. But take a deep breath now and come help me bring in some wood."

Benjie took a deep breath and went with Father to the woodpile. Beavers have a split lip that makes it possible to cut and chew under water. Benjie and Father tugged and pulled to get a branch off the frozen pile. Finally they got a nice branch loose and started toward the lodge with it. It took some twisting and turning to get it into the waterway and up into the dining room.

Benjie lay on the floor panting for breath. He was not used to staying underwater so long and working, too. His big, strong Father didn't seem to be out of breath at all.

"How can you do such hard work under the water?" asked Benjie. "I felt as though my lungs would burst."

Father was thoughtful as he answered Benjie's question. "It takes practice and patience," he said. "You can't learn everything at once." The other kits gathered around their father and brother to listen.

"Remember," continued Father, "I have been doing this for many years. When you get as old as I am, it will be easy for you. Sometimes beavers want to grow up too fast and do all the things grown-up beavers do. They find the jobs too hard for them and get discouraged. Do what you can now, and save the harder jobs for when you are older."

"You are a wonderful and wise father," said Benjie. "I want to be just like you." He gave his father a big hug and his father nuzzled him lovingly.

Mother Tells a Story

Every day now the young beavers went out into the cold water for a few minutes. They took turns helping Father get the wood from the pile of food deep in the bottom of the pond. Mother kept busy in the house, cleaning here and there, and amusing the kits with stories of the past.

"Benjie, do you know you hid behind your Mother the first time you saw me?" asked Father. "I think you were afraid of me."

"Oh, no!" exclaimed Benjie. "How could I be afraid of a wonderful Father like you?"

"Tell them, Mother," said Father, who loved to hear stories, too.

"Well, as you know, Father wasn't here when you were born. He and our older kits were washed away in the flood," began Mother. "When he came back and found us again, I didn't know what he would think about this new family of baby beavers."

Benjie sat up very straight and tried to

look important. Father gave him a little push and he rolled over.

"You two pay attention, or I'm not going to go on with the story," warned Mother.

"All right, Mother. We'll be good," promised Benjie. Father just grinned at Mother.

"When Father came swimming up the stream near that den where I had you hidden, he was glad to see me. But, being Father, he got right busy getting a dam built so we could have a pond and could build a new home."

"What were we doing?" asked a sister.

"Oh," replied Mother with a loving look, "you four kits were nestled snuggly in the den. I guess you all thought I was the only big beaver in the world."

"I guess we slept a lot," said the other sister.

"Yes, you slept a lot," answered Mother. "But then I knew it was time for you to get into the water. So I taught you to cling to my fur. We made it a game, and you soon learned to hang on tight."

"Who hung on the tightest?" asked Benjie.

"Shhh," warned the others.

"You all hung on very tight," answered Mother. "And before you knew what was happening, I dived out into the water! You let loose and bobbled and floated. How you did squeal!" Mother laughed at the memory.

"Did you teach us how to swim?" asked Benjie.

"I didn't have to. You already knew how. Swimming just comes naturally for beavers. Then Father came over to see his happy family. Benjie, when you saw another big beaver, you swam behind me and hid. You clung to my back and would not let go," said Mother.

"What did you do, Father? Did you cry?" asked Benjie.

"No," laughed Father. "I knew you would soon all love me like I loved you. I talked softly to you and gently nuzzled you and you soon learned I would not hurt you. Then you swam over and clung to my fur. And I took you down deep to the bottom of the pond."

"Oh, dear, didn't we drown?" asked Benjie.

"Of course not, silly," said his brother. "We are here, aren't we?"

"But how did we know how to

breathe?" wondered Benjie.

"Benjie, beavers have a wonderful kind of protection," Father explained. "We have little valves that close up our noses and ears when we go under water. We even have a clear, thin film that covers our eyes. We were made for the water, and these things work automatically."

"Oh," said Benjie. "Father is so smart! I am surely glad we have such a wonderful Father."

"I am glad, too," added Mother, and she fondly nuzzled Father.

"And I'm glad that I have such a good

family," said Father.

"Only one thing bad about it all," said Benjie's brother.

"What is that?" asked Father.

"We had to have a Benjie!" he replied, and then he gave a big laugh.

"You wait until we can go out in the water. I'll fix you," threatened Benjie.

"I wouldn't trade Benjie for all the world," said Mother.

"Neither would I," agreed Father. "Who would keep us laughing?"

"And who would find all the exciting things like Benjie does?" one of his sister's said and giggled.

Benjie stood up and answered, "Well, I'm glad I'm good for something."

"And don't forget, who would eat all the food if Benjie weren't here," teased his brother.

"Enough teasing for now," said Mother. "We have a lovely family, and a lovely home. We all love each other and we need each other. Let's always remember this."

The Hungry Bobcat

Early in January the biggest snow-storm of the winter came. It snowed for two days and nights. Everything was covered with a blanket of white fluffy snow. The beavers' home looked like a huge igloo coming out of the frozen pond. Everything was very beautiful in its white dress, and it was bitter, bitter cold.

Benjie and his family were snug in their home and the snow did not bother them. In fact, they probably did not even know about it. The cold weather really made their home safer. The mud on their lodge was frozen hard like cement. No enemy could get through.

The deep snow brought beauty, but it also made it hard for the animals that did not have a nice warm home as Benjie had with plenty of food. The deer trampled down the snow, making yards for them to walk around in. Rabbits had trampled down trails so they could find food. Smaller animals like the mice made little tunnels in the snow to run through and try to find food. All the animals were hungry and worked hard to find something to eat.

The larger animals were hungry, too, and probably the most hungry of all the animals was a bobcat. He had been down around Benjie's home in the fall and had given them quite a scare. They had stayed in the lodge for several days and finally the bobcat left. But now he was back looking for some fat beavers to eat.

Once in a while he would catch a mouse, but that was certainly not enough to fill a hungry bobcat. He walked on through the soft, deep snow and came to a place where several rabbits were feeding on some willows. The rabbits had made many paths among the willows and back to their homes. The bobcat smelled the fresh-peeled willow bark and seemed to know there were some animals close by. He quietly made his way toward the willows and then he saw all the rabbits hopping about in the snow trails. They were eating the peeled willow shoots.

When the bobcat saw all those delicious rabbits, his hunger pains evidently got the best of him. Instead of creeping up carefully to get the rabbits, he raced toward them. But the rabbits were not so careless. They were constantly looking all around them for enemies. Two rabbits saw the bobcat coming and they thumped a warning on the hardpacked snow trail. As if by magic, all the rabbits disappeared.

The bobcat had missed a good meal! He ran around the rabbit trails smelling and looking at the entrance ways into their homes. But there was not a rabbit to be found. Poor bobcat dropped down in the snow. He probably planned to just lie quietly in the snow and wait for the rabbits to return. Then he could get one.

But the rabbits were clever at waiting, too. They did not come out again. The sun began to sink and still the bobcat waited in the snow. He was getting colder and more hungry all the time, and still no rabbits came out. The bobcat did not give up and waited and waited.

While he was still lying in the snow, three grouse came sailing over his head in the twilight. The bobcat was so very still the birds did not notice him at all. The grouse landed in a bed of snow-covered rushes just a few feet away from him. They dug into the snow practically under his nose. Now the bobcat was getting excited again. There was a juicy supper at hand.

He would not hurry this time and scare the birds as he had the rabbits. Very slowly he crept toward them. He decided he would take two birds, one with each front paw. He was not going to miss this time!

The bobcat sprang and seized beneath the snow. Nothing! Nothing was there! How could it be? He turned at the noise of the three birds breaking through the snow in front of him and watched them fly away. The wise little birds had tunneled forward through the snow and had planned to sleep far away from their landing place.

The bobcat growled in anger and disappointment. He galloped away to another spot. He had to find something to eat! He walked along the bank of the pond. Suddenly he smelled beaver! The warm scent was coming out of the top of the beavers' lodge. He must have thought of the good taste of tender sweet meat of a young beaver and hurriedly made his way to the lodge.

Inside the lodge the Beaver family was just finishing a delightful breakfast of bark from one of the trees from the feed pile. They were chopping away and having a good time.

"What was that?" asked Benjie.

"I can't hear anything but you eating," replied his sister.

"It sounded like a scratching sound," said Benjie.

They all stopped eating to listen. Sure enough they heard a scratching noise overhead. The bobcat had found the beavers' home! They shivered as they waited. Would he be able to get them?

Benjie's Family
Faces Danger

"What do you think it is?" asked
Benjie.

"We don't have to worry," answered
Father. "No matter what it is, it cannot
break through our lodge and get in. The
cold winter has frozen the walls solid."

"But it might be a very big something," worried Benjie, "strong enough
to break in the lodge." All the young
beavers snuggled close to Mother.

"Well, even if it did, we could swim
away underwater," assured Mother.

"Listen now, the noise sounds different," whispered Benjie.

The bobcat was climbing the hollow
elm that the beavers used for a chimney.
It was here that the fresh air came in
and the stale air went out. It was from
here that the bobcat smelled the
beavers.

"Maybe a raccoon is searching for a
place to stay. Maybe he is cold," said
Benjie.

Then they heard a loud snuffling and sniffling from overhead, and a draft of air came down. In the air draft Father smelled the odor of the bobcat. He knew right away what it was. The others knew the smell meant danger. The young beavers hid behind Father and Mother, who hissed a fierce warning up the tree trunk.

When the bobcat heard the warning, it only made him more excited. Now he knew there were beavers down there. He gave an angry catlike scream and clawed fiercely at the knothole in the trunk, trying to make the opening larger. He got one paw into the hole, and a few bits of rotten wood fell down into the beavers' home.

They all jumped with fear. "You kits go into your bedroom and stay there," commanded Father. "Mother and I will stand guard. If you hear a thwack of a tail, dive into the runway and make for the water."

The young beavers huddled together in their bedroom. Benjie's sisters were almost ready to cry. "Don't make a single noise, you silly girls," warned Benjie, "or we won't be able to hear

Father thwack his tail."

"You can hear that for miles," said Benjie's brother.

"Well, I want to be sure we hear it, so let's don't talk any more," whispered Benjie.

"Mother said nothing could get in," whispered his sister.

"Bobcats have strong claws, though," whispered back the brother.

"How big are they? Could one get down in the tree?" asked the other sister.

"They are bigger than we are, but I don't know about coming down the tree," replied the brother.

"Will you all please stop talking!" whispered Benjie in a loud way.

"Benjie, can a bobcat understand beaver talk?" asked his sister.

"I don't know. I only know he can smell us and he wants to eat us," replied Benjie. "Please do be still."

"You will be eaten first because you said you were the most delicious, Benjie," reminded his brother.

"Maybe he will want to save the most delicious for last," said his sister.

"You are all talking very foolishly," said Benjie. "He is not going to get us."

"Are you sure?" asked his sister.

"Of course I am sure . . . almost," replied Benjie.

The loud scratching continued as the angry bobcat tried desperately to get into the tree. He clawed and scratched and sniffed the wonderful smell of the beaver. Mother and Father continued to hiss.

The old elm tree was too strong for the bobcat. Father had chosen a good place for their home. The bobcat rested awhile and then tried again. All night he worked on the tree, but at last he had to admit he could not get to the fat beavers, warm and snug, in their lodge. He dropped down from the tree into the deep snow. He padded slowly away from the pond, looking so very tired and disappointed.

Father noticed the odor of the bobcat was getting less and less and said quietly, "I believe he has given up at last."

"What a relief," sighed Mother. "Let's go tell the kits."

They found the kits all huddled together and sound asleep. All the excitement had made them tired.

"Poor little dears," said Mother lovingly. "They had quite a scare. But by tomorrow they will be ready for more adventures."

A Narrow Escape

The kits slept all through the day until the next night. Mother came in to see if they were all right. "My, what sleepy children I have," teased Mother and rolled them over.

"Oh, Mother, is the bobcat gone?" asked Benjie.

"Yes, he finally gave up and left," assured Mother. "I didn't think he could get through into our lodge."

"That is what I kept telling the others," bragged Benjie. "I knew he couldn't get through."

"You were just as worried as we were," said his brother.

"As you remember," Mother began, "when you were tiny you were living in a den dug out of the bank of the stream. While Father and I were building the new lodge we decided to move you to a cave nearer to where we were building the lodge."

The four kits listened carefully. They knew they were going to hear a new story about when they were little baby kits.

"I filled the cave with soft chips to make you comfortable. Then the job was to get you there. You could not walk, and I could not carry you all at once. I told Father to keep busy working on the lodge, and that I would carry you to the den. I waited until it was very dark, and then I began."

"How did you carry us?" asked Benjie. He was so excited he could hardly catch his breath.

Mother smiled. "Well, I would pick one of you up and carry you a little way and then put you down. I would go back for another kit and do the same. I kept on doing this until we were all at the cave. It took a long time, but I could not leave you too far away from me. You were sleepy and would just sleep until I came back for you. Once or twice Benjie woke up and tried to follow me. I had to give him a little cuff to make him stay put."

"I probably just wanted to help," said Benjie.

"I am sure you did, but your helps weren't always helpful," said Mother. "I just about had you all in the den, when I heard a strange sound. I could smell and feel danger."

"What was it, what was it?" cried Benjie.

"A weasel was coming toward the den.

He was really looking for mice, but he smelled you and heard you crying for me."

"Why were we crying?" asked one of the sisters.

"Well, this was a new place for you, and you didn't like all that carrying around and having your sleep disturbed," explained Mother.

"Did the weasel get close to us?" asked Benjie.

"No, I wouldn't let him. He wouldn't have eaten you. You were all too big for that. But he could hurt you, and surely he would frighten you," replied Mother.

"I charged him, and was all ready to bite him with my large, sharp teeth. When the weasel saw me, he screamed with terror and ran deep into the woods. I doubt if he tried to make a dinner of beaver kits again." Mother was enjoying her own story.

"What a narrow escape!" exclaimed Benjie. "You are almost as good a fighter as Father."

"Indeed she is!" Father laughed. He gave Mother a big smile.

"But she is also the sweetest, most loving Mother any beaver could have," declared Benjie.

"That she is too," agreed Father. They all went over and gave Mother a big hug. Mother smiled happily at her family.

Playing Tag
with Father

"Will we ever have warm weather again?" wondered Benjie.

"Yes, we will," replied Mother. "Then we will have plenty of work to do to keep us busy."

"I will be glad for that," said Benjie as he stretched. "I get tired of staying in the lodge all the time."

"Why don't you kits go explore all the waterways. Maybe you will find something interesting," suggested Mother.

"May we go out into the pond, too?" asked Benjie.

"No," said Mother, "not unless Father is with you. If you find him, maybe he will take you for a little swim."

The beavers were quickly off to find Father. They swam in and out of the waterways that led to the pond and to the lodge and finally they found him. "Father, Father, will you take us for a swim?" called the kits.

Father looked at the four beaver kits and laughed. "So you are all full of energy and have nothing to do. All right, come with me. See if you can catch me." With that Father gave a quick dive out of the lodge and swam swiftly in the water.

The kits squealed with delight at this game and bumped into each other trying to get out of the lodge. When they got out,

Father was not to be seen. They swam all around, looking and looking. They finally had to go back into the lodge for a breath of air. There sat Father waiting for them.

"Why, where have you been?" he asked.

"What kind of a game of tag is that?"

asked Benjie's brother. "We couldn't even find you."

"Why, then we will have to try again," called Father as he dived into the water and out of the lodge.

"Let's go," they shouted and once again they tumbled out of the lodge. This time Father let them see him a little bit then swam swiftly away. The kits knew he would not go far, for they could not hold their breath as long as he could. They darted here and there as fast as their bodies would go, but they could not find Father. Once again they had to make their way back into the lodge and there was Father calmly combing his fur.

"Do you live here?" asked Father, looking serious.

"Oh, Father, you know we do!" They all laughed. "Come play a real game of tag with us."

"Very well," he said. "Come, we will all go into the water together." This time they all went out into the pond together. Father tagged Benjie and swam away. Benjie tried to catch Father, but decided his brother would be easier. He swam up to him and gave his tail a gentle nip, and then swam away. His brother turned quickly, but Benjie was too fast for him.

His brother began to chase his sister when all of a sudden Father appeared in front of him. He gave Father a gentle tap with his tail, then all the kits headed for the lodge. They each took a different tunnel and all came sputtering into the main room at the same time. Father was last this time. The kits laughed and laughed.

"I guess Father must have gotten tagged in the game," said Mother.

"Yes, I did," replied Father. "And then they all left me outside to drown."

"You funny Father!" Benjie laughed lovingly. "You wouldn't drown and you know it. We just wanted to beat you inside for once."

"Now who is going to help me bring in some food so we can have a snack?" asked Father.

"I will," they all cried out at once.

"I only need one beaver," said Father.

"Let my brother go," said Benjie.

So Father and Benjie's brother went out into the icy water once more to get something to eat. It wasn't long until they were back. They all had a good snack, and then Mother told them to do a good job of combing and oiling their fur.

The beaver is very careful to take care of his fur and make sure it is waterproof. The young beavers are taught to care for their fur, and Benjie knew just how to do it.

First he pressed all the water from his fur coat with his front claw paws. Then he used his hind webbed feet for combing. The second toe on each large hind foot has a special split claw, just right for combing the water from thick fur and spreading the oil over the hairs from tiny oil sacs in their skin. Benjie used this claw to comb and comb and comb. He did not hurry, but took all the time he needed to make his coat shiny and clean.

Who would have thought underneath all that snow and ice there was a family of beavers so busy playing tag in the icy water and living a happy life! Every day the sun was brighter and the weather got warmer and winter was beginning to leave the pond.

Exploring under Ice

A cracking sound rang out over the pond, and then another, and another. It was a new sound to Benjie and he wondered what it was.

"Father, I hear a different sound," said Benjie. "Do you know what it is?"

"Does it sound as if something is cracking?" asked Father.

"Why, yes, it does, now that you mention it. Do you think our lodge is cracking?" asked Benjie.

"No, you don't have to worry about that. It is the ice on the pond outside. I imagine the warm sun shining on it is causing it to crack," said Father.

"Do you mean the ice is all melted and we can go out into the fresh air?" asked Benjie, all excited at the thought.

"Hold on now, young fellow," Father answered. "You are rushing things. It will be some time before old man sun makes all that ice melt. It is very thick and hard. But at least it is beginning." Then Father added, "Call the others and we will swim out and inspect the cracks."

Benjie quickly went to find his brother and sisters and Mother. "Hurry, hurry," he called, "we are going out to see the cracks."

"The what?" asked his brother.

"The cracks in the ice on the pond, you dummy," explained Benjie.

"And who made you so wise?" answered his brother.

"You know Father has been telling him things again, and then Benjie acts as though he knows everything," said his sister as she laughed.

"No, I don't," retorted Benjie. "Can I help it because I am smart and learn quickly?"

"Let's call him Benjamin Extra Bright Beaver," suggested his sister.

"Are you going to stand around and argue all day or go out in the pond?" asked Mother. She turned and dived into one of the waterways that led to the pond and the other beavers quickly followed.

Father led them up to the surface to look for the cracks. In some places you could see them, but in other places the ice was too thick for the crack to come all the way through. The beavers put their noses up to the cracks and tried to see through. But they could not. They stayed out as long as they could hold their breath and then swam back into the lodge.

"I thought there would be some big openings in the ice," said Benjie disappointed. "The cracks are just jagged lines."

"Just be patient, Benjie," replied Father. "Soon all the ice will be all broken up, and we will be out in the fresh air again."

"Could we go out again to see who can find the longest crack?" asked Benjie, who liked to make a game out of everything.

"All right," agreed Father, "but remember to save enough breath to get back into the lodge." The young beavers swam in and out of the lodge many times, examining the cracks. Once Benjie had hit his nose against the ice and it cracked right then and there. The loud noise frightened him and he tried to thwack his tail underwater and dive. It was a funny, clumsy movement. When he got back into the lodge, the other beavers laughed at him.

"What kind of a trick was that you did, Benjie?" asked his brother.

"I'll bet you couldn't do it," replied Benjie, who didn't want to admit he had been frightened.

"I am sure I wouldn't want to," replied his brother.

"I think you have been in the water long enough," said Mother. "Why don't you each go out and get a small piece of wood and bring it back to the lodge. You need to sharpen your teeth."

Beavers' teeth grow all the time and must be used often to wear them down.

Soon all the beavers were back, each with a piece of wood. They sat in the big room of the lodge and chewed away at the wood. They liked to do this. First they peeled off all the bark, and ate it. Then they cut up the wood into tiny pieces.

"Don't forget to clean up all the mess when you are finished," said Mother.

"We won't," answered the kits. It was as much fun to clean up the mess as it was to make it. They gathered up all the pieces and carried them out into the water into the pond. The pieces floated away down the stream under the ice.

Benjie Is Foolish

A whole week had passed since Benjie heard the ice cracking. Every day the beavers went out to inspect the cracks to see if the ice had opened up any. They were so anxious to see outside again and breathe fresh air.

"You know, I'll bet I could break that ice," said Benjie thoughtfully. "If I got way down deep in the pond and zoomed up and hit it, I am sure it would break."

"I don't think you'd better try it without first asking Father," warned his brother.

"Oh, Father doesn't want us to stay babies all our lives," replied Benjie. "We have to learn to think for ourselves."

"Still, it is best to ask him about things like that," his brother said.

"Well, you go ask," answered Benjie, "but I am going to try."

He went back into the lodge and got a big breath of air and then dived out of the lodge deep into the pond. He gave a mighty shove through the water and aimed at the ice. His nose hit it with a bang! Benjie was knocked back into the water, but the ice was just as solid as ever. The hard smack almost knocked Benjie out, and he floated dizzily in the

water. His brother saw he needed help and grabbed hold of his fur and pulled him into the lodge.

Benjie lay on the floor of the lodge panting and holding his nose. "Oh, oh, it hurts!" he cried.

"Why, Benjie, how did you hurt your nose?" asked Mother.

Benjie's brother told the whole story, and Benjie felt so very foolish. It had sounded like a good idea at first, but now it seemed very silly. Father came in to inspect his nose and love him a little.

"It will be sore for a while," said Father sympathetically, "but I think you will live to tell the tale."

"I don't think he will want to tell about this very often," said his sister.

"Benjamin," Father said sternly but lovingly, "it is too bad you have to learn these lessons the hard way. You know you could have broken your teeth. That would have been a tragedy. Beavers just can't live without their teeth."

"He said you would want him to think for himself," said his sister.

"Yes, I do," replied Father, "but I expect you kits to think of the right things to do. And if it is dangerous, you should think of the results. Benjie didn't think long enough so now he has to suffer."

Mother was listening carefully, then she said, "I know it has been a long winter for you young beavers, but it takes time for the spring to come. Just think of all the animals that do not have a lovely, safe home as we do. Think, too, of all the animals that have to go hunt for their food every day, and maybe not find any. We have our food right by us and we can always have something to eat. I am glad we can stay in out of the cold all winter."

"Oh, I am glad, too," said Benjie. "I am sorry I did such a foolish thing. Thank you, Brother, for bringing me in."

"Oh, that is all right," his brother answered. "I was wishing the trick would work. But Mother is right. It is best to wait for the ice to break by itself."

"When we get out again, there won't be much time for stories," Mother said. "You will all want to be playing in the water anyway."

"And I have a special big project for the young beavers this spring," said Father mysteriously. "They might not even have time for play."

"What is it?" cried all the beavers.

"I'm not going to tell you now. You will just have to wait for the warm weather to come," answered Father.

"We have a lot of surprises for you," added Mother with a faraway look in her eye.

"Will we like them?" asked Benjie.

"Indeed you will," said Mother. "All beavers like surprises."

"Benjie, you'd better take your battle-scarred nose and go to bed," said Father.

"What is a battle scar?" asked Benjie.

"It is a hurt when you get in a fight," said Father laughingly.

"Benjie had a fight with the ice," teased his brother.

"I really wasn't fighting and neither was the ice," answered Benjie.

"But the ice won anyway," said his brother.

"Someday I will tell you about some of my battle scars," promised Father.

"Oh, goody," they all cried.

"But now it is time for bed and rest," reminded Mother.

The kits went into their bedroom and curled up for sleep.

"Does your nose hurt very much?" whispered his sister.

"It is much better now, thank you," replied Benjie.

"You may put your head on me if it will help," said his sister. Benjie curled up close to his sister and was soon sound asleep.

Father's Battle Scars

When Benjie woke up the next day, the first thing he did was to gently feel his nose. It did feel much, much better. Then he remembered that Father promised to tell them about his battle scars.

"Wake up, everyone. Let's go find Father so he can tell us his adventures," called Benjie.

The kits all tumbled out of bed and hurried to find Father. Father was already up and had been out to the feed pile. He had brought in a delicious piece of wood for breakfast. He and Mother had already started to eat.

"Well how is our nosey beaver this morning?" asked Father.

"My nose feels much better, thank you," replied Benjie.

"We want to hear about your battle scars," said Benjie's brother.

"When we finish eating, Father can tell you about his adventures," Mother promised.

As usual the meal was a noisy, happy one. In a short time breakfast was over.

The beavers gathered around Father, and he soon began his story. "This happened before the new lodge was built. You were still in your burrow in the side of the bank of the river that Mother had dug out. There was only one waterway to this hole, but it was enough, since Mother was the only one going in and out. You were still too young to leave the nest. Mother was taking care of you when suddenly there appeared a strange beaver in the entrance of the burrow. This stranger had broken the beavers' law by coming into another beaver's pond. To come right into a mother's nest with babies was even worse. Mother hissed and flew at him in a rage. She drove him out of the burrow into the pond. Then she gave a loud thwack with her tail, and hurried back into the burrow to protect you."

"Oh, what a brave mother!" exclaimed Benjie.

"But Father is braver," added Mother. "He heard my thwack and came to my rescue. You should have seen how frightened that beaver looked when he saw Father."

"What did you do, Father?" eagerly asked the kits.

"I leaped on his back, slashed through his beaver fur with my sharp teeth in the right place where I would break his backbone."

Father got excited just telling about the big fight. "He fought desperately, biting and snarling," he continued. "But I was very angry at him for coming into my pond and bothering Mother and you kits. And when a beaver is angry, he is very strong!"

Father straightened up and, adding a few gestures with his fists, continued. "He dived to the bottom of the pond, but I held on to him, and we churned and rolled in the pool. How we did fight! The water was turning red with blood."

"Did you win?" asked Benjie excitedly. The kits' eyes were wide open with admiration.

"Well," said Father, "I can't really say who won because that stranger finally got away from me and swam to the edge of the pond and went as fast as he could far away from the pond. We certainly never saw him again. I hurried back to

Mother to see if she and the kits were all right. And you were."

"Oh, you should have seen him!" said Mother. "He was all covered with cuts, and I was so worried. I made him rest for three days before I would let him do any work."

"And she brought me tender leaves to eat and watched over me." Father looked fondly at Mother. "She was such a good nurse. If my cuts hadn't hurt so much, it would have been fun to be hurt."

"You silly husband," said Mother. "You were up and around again and working as hard as ever by the fourth day."

"Only because you took such good care of me," assured Father.

"But where are the battle scars?" asked Benjie. "I can't see them."

"No, you can't, Benjie. They are under my thick fur," Father told the kits. "The fur grows back over them and you would never know I had had a battle. But they are there. Do you want to dig down into the fur and try to find them?"

As quick as a flash, the kits scrambled all over Father and began to poke into his deep fur looking for the scars.

Father laughed and jiggled all around. "You are tickling me. Stop, stop!"

"Maybe someday I'll have some battle scars of my own," said Benjie.

"You might at that," answered Father, "but I hope you don't have to have any rough battles like I have had. Let's go out for a little swim under the ice."

Floating on Ice

Father came swimming into the lodge all excited. "Hurry, hurry everyone! Come with me. I have a wonderful surprise for you!"

Mother and the kits hurried to the waterways and they swam out with Father. They swam under water for a while and then suddenly Father went up to the top. They all followed and before they realized what had happened, they had their heads out of water.

"Oh, oh, the ice has broken!" cried Benjie.

"Fresh air!" they all cried and they breathed and breathed.

"The ice isn't all gone, of course," said Father. "It will take some time for it all to melt and float away. But it broke first here by the dam. We can climb up here and sit for awhile."

The beavers all climbed upon the icy dam and sat down. What a picture they made as they sat there with their tails hanging in the water. Father went to the shore of the pond and brought back some branches for them to chew on. It was indeed a nice outdoor party for the beavers.

"My tail is getting cold," complained Benjie.

"That's because it has no fur on it," said Mother. "Tuck it under you and sit on it. That will keep it warm." She showed them how to do it. The kits looked even funnier sitting on their tails along the top of the dam.

"I almost forgot how things looked around our lodge," remarked Benjie.

"Well, we didn't have too much time to explore," said Father. "We were so busy building the lodge and bringing in wood to the feed pile before the winter came that we didn't have much time for play. But now that spring is surely on its way, we will have more time to get acquainted with everything."

"I wonder if you can see where the bobcat scratched on our tree," said Benjie's brother. "I am going to look for that when I can go all over the place."

"One word of warning," Father said firmly. "Be careful when you come up out of the water. The sharp edges of the floating ice could cut you. You aren't tough like your old father."

"May we play around a little now?" asked Benjie.

"Yes," answered Father, "but do be careful."

The kits dived back into the water and played hide-and-seek under the ice. Benjie found a big chunk of ice floating in the stream. He climbed upon it and was soon sailing along on his make-believe boat. "Look at me, look at me!" shouted Benjie. "I am floating."

The brother and sisters thought of a trick to play on Benjie. They silently swam under the block of ice and put their paws on one side and pushed up. The block of ice tipped and Benjie went sliding into the water.

"Beaver overboard!" called all the young beavers. Benjie came sputtering to the top. "That was fun," he called. "Let's do it again."

The trick was soon turned into a beaver game. They took turns riding the ice and tipping each other off into the water. Beavers are such happy creatures and love to play. They can turn almost anything, even work, into play.

"Time to come in," called Mother. "You can't stay out too long in this cold weather. Take a good, deep breath and come in. We'll go out again tomorrow."

The beavers all swam into the lodge and were soon busy pressing the cold water out of their fur and combing it.

"Just to know that we can go out every day makes me so happy," said Benjie.

"Will the surprise you have for us start right away, Father?" asked Benjie's brother.

"No, we will have to wait for all of the ice to melt," said Father. "It will have to be much warmer than it is now. Don't worry, we will have time for it."